Beasts

of

Man

BY
Haven Shin

Beasts of Man

∩

The sun burns. Actually, the sun makes me shine but sets my skin on fire. Scorches like Hell fire. The wind combs my beard but can't soothe my skin. Doesn't matter, not much I can do about it. This ain't nothing to me. Besides, I have work to do. I grab my axe, squeeze, and keep splittin' logs for firewood.

I walked along the familiar trail, pulling logs from behind in a fatigued rustic sled. Towering trees create the perfect path for me. The sun illuminated bits of the ground through thick leaves above. The whole path was the same: earthy brown mud with many branches and rocks to step on. Without thinking or looking, I know where to place my feet. It was like the ground was molded to my foot. But every trip I'd find something that would jab into the soles of my bare feet. At night I would keep time that way, examining the scratches, marks, and scars.

When I finally got to the trailer park, everything felt familiar. Everything was where it was supposed to be. Felt safe, quiet. Most of the cars were sun bleached shells, with plenty of rust. You could tell which way the sun was positioned by looking at the paint. Every car had splotches of color in one lone spot on its body. Rust covered the tops and seemed to be trying to find a path to work its way down to the roots. But there was one truck by the entrance that kept most of its color after all this time. The hood stood locked into place. Most of its organs were picked clean, and its back was completely covered in a flaky reddish brown. Dried blood on his back I'd say. The dirt could barely hold its weight. Still, the sun couldn't fully strip the truck naked. His face kept the brightest blue color in the whole trailer park. Every day, the trailer park is more covered in rust, but this one truck was still blue.

"Still ain't dead yet, I see. Me neither, me neither," I muttered to the truck but more for myself. I had no real use for talking, but it reminded me that I was still here.

Outside each trailer, there are tables and chairs with missing legs, dirt, cracks, and leftover cans and coolers. I picked the trailer clean of food long ago. I still remember the first time I saw a metal can. I could not make out the characters on it, but it was clear what was inside—beans. It took me days to figure out how to open it. I tossed it against a tree to see if that would work. All I did was leave a huge dent, but it still would not open. I finally opened it with a sharp rock, smashing the top of the can until it spilled on the ground. Eventually, I realized I could split the can in two with my ax. It was how I ate before there were no more cans.

In the center of the cars was a stone pit of black burnt wood and ashes. Song sparrows singing, squirrels scurrying, and deer prancing, I was unbothered hearing all their sounds, having been here for many years.

The sun was going down, so I tried to make a fire. I gathered all the wood together and threw it in the pre-made pit. I reached into my pocket for matches but felt nothing. I looked in all the coolers for matches, but none were found. I sat facing the pit. Fresh wood became less distinguishable from old as it got darker. I picked sticks and tried rubbing them together to start a spark, but nothing happened. Some days, I could make a fire with ease. Today was not one of them, so I tried to get as comfortable as I could get and tried to sleep.

As I lay looking at the sky, I saw only pitch black. I knew the thick olive bristles covered the moonlight, yet the moon didn't want to shine on me. I'm used to lying on my back and resting my head on the earth. Each night is different from the one before. Some nights, the rough, jagged terrain becomes a soft, smooth bed. I wore a shirt, expecting the breeze to pick up and temperatures to drop. Winds didn't affect me, though; the shirt was making it worse. I tossed it to the side. The wind was soothing and warming on my skin. I wasn't comfortable, but I laid in peace and silence.

This home was my only comfort in all the years of being alone.

***

Our journey up the mountains had been harsh. My crew and I, who are stationed near the foot of the mountain, have been tracking a mysterious beast deep within the forest. There have been reports by our hunters that a wild creature was viciously murdering the deer and rabbits in the forest. The way the carcasses laid mangled and half-chewed suggest that this was not the work of a human. This tracks as our camp haven't seen another human outside of our own community in years. Some eyewitness accounts thought it was a big bear; others insisted it was a yeti or a sasquatch. Regardless, the beast remains elusive. The hunters have even become too afraid to hunt, costing us valuable food and supplies.

Our expedition has lasted months, and we still haven't found the creature yet. However, the night before, we had noticed something strange—many of the footsteps we found looked oddly human shaped. But it didn't make sense for a man to be able to walk this rough terrain without any shoes. It made even less sense that a human would survive the harsh climate here for long. The large minerals on the ground were jagged enough to cut through regular sneakers. Many of my men had to wear heavy leather boots to even walk on the terrain.

We eventually made our way to the top of the mountain successfully, yet the beast stayed hidden. Not one direct sighting in this whole time. We decided to give up on the search and return home. There was no chance for a successful continuation of the expedition with morale, resources, and rations depleting. We lost far too many men along the way. About two months into our expedition, our rations began to steadily drain, so we were forced to institute a strict rationing system—one can of food for every two men. However, some of the men decided to seek nourishment elsewhere in the woods. They discovered a rich, glistening liquid among the branches scattered on the ground. Famished and thinking it was sap, they drank it without much thought. They all quickly became ill and died within the week. Others succumbed to the elements, found curled into a ball and frozen. Some were even mysteriously found at the bottom of cliffs. The expedition started as a crew of 20 men; now, it was whittled down to five, including me.

The sun began to set, bleeding its final light on the final day of this cursed expedition. I stopped the group in a pocket between the trees with enough space to create a fire. I carried the freshly cut firewood over, splinters sticking out of the middle where the cuts were made. I threw all the firewood together in the center of the little space we had. The fire blossomed, bringing a comforting heat that wrapped us all in a blanket. I looked around at the little circle gathered around the fire. I looked around at my remaining crew, disheveled but still had some life in them. I also noticed that there was an abandoned trailer park next to us. It was clear life ended here long ago, so not worth investigating. We barely survived the trip, which makes the chances of anyone surviving extremely low. Instead, focused on the flames and each other. It brought a symbol of hope that everyone desperately needed, a beacon for us all. Now, all we needed to do was to make our way back home in the morning.

***

Suddenly, a fearsome, intense light through the rows of trunks and bundles of bushes startled me awake. Who's here? Someone, or *someones*, must be here trying to kill me. They want my home and want to take it from me.

Like hell they will.

I sprinted to the light. I held my axe tight and tried to dodge each branch and log in my way. I swung the axe around, chopping down branches in my way. But I was getting tired. I stopped, sweating and frantically panting. I dropped the axe, got on all fours and slithered through the woods. Everything was easier to dodge now. Every step felt more natural. I moved quicker and quicker the closer I got to the light. My hands stamped on the earth. My feet right after.

I stopped. I stood on my legs. Above the bushes, I peered closer at the light. A smoky fog screened the stars. I took a long inhale and felt a stabbing pain impale my chest: the sweet, tangy scent sprinkled with the bits of ash in the air. It worked its way into my lungs, etching new scars. I tried to exhale, but my body shook, and I started coughing uncontrollably. Something was stabbing the inside of my throat. I can't breathe. Weakened, I collapsed to my knees. I tried to clear my throat, but nothing happened. But then I heard noises in the direction of the light. I started running on my hands and feet again towards the light.

I waited behind bushes, creeping closer to catch a glimpse of the fire starters. I could see the smoke rising from the light. I could see the glow through the bushes I hid behind. A raging mini sun brighter than a red cardinal, with a blinding heavenly glow.

The five men talk funny. I couldn't make out a word they said. Looking at them, they seemed weak and cut up all over their bodies. Some of the cuts looked deep, others missing fingers and even a whole hand. Their stuff was in a pile behind the tents. Maybe they have food that I can take after I'm done with them. I scurried over. I squinted through the dark towards their bags. The men were further, unrecognizable from here.

I tried to focus on the stuff, but I could not ignore them as their voices grew louder. They talk mad. Even their laughs sound mad. What came out of their mouths made me know what I already think must've been true. I'm right. They are here to kill me. And they won't.

I crawled through a small opening near their equipment. The front side of my body dragged against the barbed branches. Warm blood flowed like a river down my body. I carefully made my way to the bags in front. I reached for a strap and lost balance, banging my head into the ground. Thick, tepid liquid began to choke me. Rich red blood surged as I opened my mouth.

***

Moments before I was about to drift into sleep, we all heard it and jumped into action. What was that sudden bang? We all froze for a while, staring at each other and communicating without making any noise. The flame continued to scorch, growing stronger with the winds beating up on the leaves. We all listened for the sound to happen again. A bit of rustling came from behind me, near the tents. I gave a nod, a signal, for someone to check out the noise. He crept towards the tent with a spoon in one hand, everyone staring as he got closer. The rustling became louder, and others began raising their spoons and pots to prepare for whatever it was. I clenched my pocketknife behind my back and slowly stood up. I raised the knife in front of me, ready for an attack, ready to strike. As he reached the bags, his body was tense, grasping onto the spoon high up in the air. With each trembling step, I thought he would lose his balance. My chest was thumping, sweat dripped, blurring the knife's reflection of myself shaking rapidly. Every muscle in my body stiffened until I saw his shoulders drop. He let his arm go and turned back around.

"Guys, it's nothing. It's just a squirrel or something. Everything is—"

Bang!

***

So many screams around me. I didn't know what had just happened. I just grabbed something, this small, shiny object. I pointed it in the air to examine what it was, and then all of the sudden a loud sound occurred. I dropped to the ground, and I peeked my head above the bags. I saw the man on his knees. His eyes were hollow. Blood was spilling out of his mouth like a ghastly maroon, spilling out of his chest, gushing everywhere. There, that's where it was coming from, that small hole in his chest. The hole was deeper than any cut I ever got, and I could see the blood inching down, pooling on the ground beneath him. All the other men were running towards him. I looked down, and in my hands lay this metal object that made the ear-piercing noise. I noticed how light it felt between my hands. I had no idea such a small object could be so powerful. As the men circled around him, one looked up, yelling and pointing towards me. They were going to kill me now, I knew it. I pointed the metal object in their direction. My finger danced around the object, searching for a way to make that loud sound again.

Bang!

***

My ears, now ringing from the echoing screams all around, felt numb after the second gunshot. I tried to rub my ears but couldn't feel anything. I looked down at my hand, and there was blood. So much blood. The side of my head began to heat up, but I stared at the rich red wine liquid covering my hands. I could feel the heat of losing my ear spreading through my body, yet there wasn't any pain. The numbing was soothing, making me want to just stand in place. I could see someone trying to grab my attention. He appeared to be screaming, but all I could feel were the vibrations through the soles of my feet. He pointed at his back, then back at me, repeatedly. I turned my head over my shoulder, and a rush of heat blinded me. There was no sensation of any heat on my face, but I couldn't see out of my right eye anymore. I couldn't even feel my heart beating in my chest. My body was just cold and numb.

Bang!

***

Power, power, power. I understand how this weapon works now. All you have to do is squeeze that little piece and it makes a boom. The men will fall if I squeeze the object in front of them. *Who's next?* I looked around at all these men scurrying around like insects. One was on the ground, crawling, like a caterpillar, towards another who stood still whilst dancing with the flames. Two lay motionless on the ground, blood flowing from their bodies like rivers connecting into one body of blood. Three men remained. They kept their distance from me. I think they understood the power I have. A single and blinding light spread everywhere. It lay on the men, the pit, the bags, and the tents. The heavens had come down to smile on me.

Bang! Bang!

Now's my chance. I dropped the metal weapon and dashed towards the trailer park.

***

I looked around and saw all my men. Some lay motionless while a couple were doing the death rattle. Whether they were alive or dead, everywhere, everywhere I looked, I could see blood pouring from their bodies. I saw the tears that were streaming down their cheeks, and the unanswered prayers for the pain to end. Flames raged around us, with everything being burned to ash. I prayed to die too, join my comrades, and get sent out of this hell. Yet, I was somehow the only one who was still alive. Face-to-face with this—this creature was no beast, but a man—a man who wanted to kill us all. I was the last one standing.

***

As I ran, I felt a presence behind me. I looked at the light behind me and saw a figure standing amid it all. The figure seemed to have no clothes but was approaching slowly. There was an intense glow that bordered the figure. This figure felt different from the men that were trying to kill me. Something told me to stay, so I stopped running, turned around, and waited for the figure to approach me. It was a tall, immense beacon of comfort. It felt non-threatening, and its blinding hue gave a sense of hope and power, lighting the dark forest that encompassed us. I began to approach the figure.

***

I spotted the dark figure lurking in the shadows of the woods. The moonlight from behind outlined the slim form, snow white. I began approaching it. Blood poured from my body as rich Tuscan wine from a bottle glass. I felt myself growing weaker with every step. I was losing too much blood, but I won't let him get away. Even if I bled out after this was all over, I would be ok with this. Whether I live or die, this ends now.

As I passed the forest line, the branches bit into my clothes, tearing them apart. Bite after bite, shreds of my shirt and pants wafted to the floor until there was no more to bite off. I continued without hesitation while the branches continued to claw at me. The pain was torturous, unforgiving, yet no thoughts of stopping came over me. I could see the flesh on my arms, expanded by each branch. It had the marbling of a New York strip steak, the ivory fat with the apple red muscle, and more and more of my flesh was being exposed.

The figure began walking towards me. I started to hear the cries of my men, screams that you should only hear in the depths of hell. Or the war. These men fought in the war with me. We all nearly died together many times. We saw the same corpses, the same pools of blood, the same screams. Men, women, and children. Yet, we somehow survived it all. We thought death and destruction was behind us. Now, they were no different than the bodies in the battlefield. They had the same dried tears and the same unanswered prayers as the light from the fire glistened on them. Their eyes radiated, removed from the safety and security they'd have if they were given a chance to be closed.

***

Once he got close enough to me, I saw that the figure was a man, one of the men by the fire. He stopped walking towards me. He stood there. Two deathly eyes glowing. Slowly, he descended below the bushes. I couldn't see him, but I felt an intense pressure. Like something was behind me, drooling down my neck. I was being hunted, stalked like prey. Looking at his eyes, I knew he wasn't trying to eat me. He did not want to take my home away from me. All he wanted was me, and only me, dead. This tall, immense man was no longer a man but a predator. He is a beast.

***

My blood boiled. My body was steaming. I wanted this coward to fear, scream, and plead with me. I lusted for his blood. What would his wine taste like? Light, bold, fruity, or earthy? My mouth began to flood, oozing saliva, dripping onto the floor.

***

I felt my chest drumming faster and faster. The beat was overtaking my thoughts. THUMP, THUMP, THUMP, THUMP. I looked around frantically for this beast. I couldn't see anything. I spotted the light ahead and immediately sprinted towards it.

***

The fear, the urgency, how it danced in my nostrils. As I inhaled deeply, I could smell the sweat racing down his body. My ears perked up, and I could hear the terror in each frantic step. A rush came over me, and all my pain was gone. I bent down and got on all fours. Like a wolf hungry for its next meal, I chased the critter.

***

I looked around for the beast. The bushes around me violently rustled. The fire began to die, with the light fading along with it.

***

I circled steadily, hawking my prey down. I could see his blood flowing down his front. I began to salivate.

***

I picked up a metal weapon off the ground and held it in front of me. It was visibly shaking, and I couldn't stop it. Every muscle in my body tensed up, yet still shaking.

***

The light was nearly gone, and I could only see the outline of his figure. I dug my hands into the earth, preparing to pounce. I readjusted and felt something metallic.

***

The light vanished. Even with the powerful weapon, each beat weakened me. THUMP. THUMP. THUMP. I couldn't feel anything else. I couldn't hear anything else. Everything began to shake.

***

I couldn't feel anything. Everything was silent. I raised the gun from the ground and laid my finger on the trigger.

***

My sweat was dripping profusely, and I felt weak. My eyes shifted—left, then right, right, then left.

A crack behind me.

***

I sprang out of the bushes–

***

I swiftly spun around.

***

"DIE, BEAST!" they yelled.

BANG! BANG!

***

The sun beamed into my eyes. Am I dead? Is this Heaven? But, once I opened my eyes, I saw the ash from last night's fire, the bodies of my men, the gun, the beast. No, I am somehow alive.

I tried to get up, but a sharp pain shot through my body. I looked at my arm, which was a burned and mangled mess. I touched around my face and felt a piece of my ear missing. I looked around and saw him again. He looked less fearsome in the sunlight. He was no beast or yeti like we all thought. He was just a man, a pathetic frail man. As I stared at the bullet hole between his eyes, I couldn't help but be disgusted by what I saw. His clothes were in tatters and his feet were permanently stained black from never wearing shoes.

"This is all your fault. You did this to me, you did this to my men. We weren't your enemy, so why?"

Why. I don't remember the last time I asked myself this question. Just when things were starting to make sense, after everything we all went through, he had to come along and destroy everything. Now, my blood boiled with the thought that I now needed answers.

"The war is long over. Come on, I know that. You know that. My buddies lying on the ground knew that. At least, you should've known that. God, how stupid are you? Didn't we kill enough people back then? Half of us, gone in an instant. Half the world's population, and you just thought it would make no difference to kill five more, didn't you. Well, you were right in the end. Except you didn't expect to be one of the five. I'm still here."

No answer. What was I thinking? Of course he can't answer, he's dead. And that's it. He's not going to fight back, defend himself, tell me that I'm the one who's wrong. I'm the real monster in this fight.

"You know what? Screw you. I have a community to look after. Sure, we rebuilt, but it still isn't what it used to be. We have electricity and running water, but we still have to hunt for food every day. But you only cared about yourself. You can steal our food and scare our hunters just so you can eat? We take in refugees, we have women and children to look after. You just think that the world revolves around you. You really believe that there aren't any consequences to your actions."

"I take back what I said. You were my enemy. I killed you because I hated you. You stole food from my dinner table. You stole fathers from their children. You left me with this mess to clean up. If you came back to life right now, I'd kill you again. I don't care what excuses you have. You chose your life and destroyed ours. You killed us and now I have to bury my dead. Not that you would know anything about that."

I looked him dead in the eyes as I said my piece. However, I noticed that the sun was getting brighter, and the temperature was beginning to rise. I need to get going if I am going to make it back before it gets dark.

Almost all of our supplies were destroyed, but I managed to find a shovel. I didn't have the strength to bury them properly, but I had to do something to honor them. They were good men, with lives and families. Proper men who didn't deserve this. Real men. There wasn't much to mark the grave, but I placed some rocks and wilted flowers on top to give my men some of the dignity they deserved. I gave a silent prayer, though I still didn't have the words to make sense of all of this. I looked one last time at our killer.

"No one is going to pray for you, least of all me."

I spat on him and turned towards the road. I tossed my shovel aside and turned towards the camp, trying to find any supplies that I could use for my journey home.

As I walked down the path, it became clear that I was more injured than I realized. I could not get a solid footing, and I kept slipping on the moist ground. Just when I thought I had acclimated myself to the path, I fell faced first into the mud. My clothes were starting to become shredded from the sharp branches. When we came up, we had equipment, and we could clear any path. Now, I was just as pathetic as the monster in the trailer park.

***

How long has it been since our patrol team left to go hunt the bear? Days, maybe even months even. I trained for this scenario, but none of this feels real. Twenty men, our best and most skilled, some of them even fought in the war, have gone missing after searching for a bear. One single bear. Sure, this bear was ferocious enough to scare off the hunters, but this should have been nothing for those men. But they still haven't returned, and the council organized a search party. I've only been training for a few months, but I needed to know what happened, so I volunteered. Besides, there aren't many other men left that even know how to shoot.

The hunters leading the party are frustratingly cautious. "We saw the beast, we must tread carefully," they kept repeating, almost like they were trying to remind themselves. We kept close to each other, scanning the perimeter before even taking a single step. Every so often, I would look behind me. Yep, I can still see the entrance to our camp.

Before long, everyone had a theory about what happened. I kept quiet, trying to get the group to pick up the pace.

"I'm telling you guys—it's not a bear, it's a yeti. We should've brought bigger guns with us"

"That's ridiculous. There's a more logical explanation for everything. We just hunted on land we should have stayed away from. I told the council we should never expand our hunting radius. You guys must've stepped on some ancient burial ground and now we're cursed."

"It could still be a yeti, though. Didn't one of you say that you heard a scream when you went hunting. Like, almost human sounding?"

"The sound was from ancient ghosts. I'm telling you."

The group leader, a man who was old, but who somehow spoke like he was older, finally had enough of all the speculations. He clearly didn't want to be outside of the camp any longer than he needed to be, and he was tired of playing babysitter.

"Christ, why did we have to have kids on the search party? You do realize that there are plenty of animals that sound like humans if you're not paying attention. I fought in the war, you know? I know what a human scream sounds like and that wasn't it. You kids have never seen a dead rabbit let alone piles of human corpses on the battlefield. It's a bear. A. Bear. No more discussion. Focus on the mission."

18

Before any objections could be raised, we heard a gunshot. It was hard to tell where it came from. Everyone immediately stopped and looked at each other.

"None of us shot our guns, right?"

"No, did you?"

"Nah. I think it came from the woods"

"Of course, it came from the woods ... your ears would be ringing otherwise. I'm supposed to be leading a rescue party, not babysitting. Get your guns at the ready. Spread out like we trained. We're walking into the woods."

***

I patted myself to make sure I wasn't hit. I can't believe that I missed that rock sticking out along the path. I can't believe that I fell in a way that my gun went off. I slowly pick myself up. Luckily, I didn't twist my ankle during the fall. It was difficult to be certain in these woods, but I felt close to camp. I followed the path, I kept track of how much time had passed. I looked up and noticed the sun peeking through the trees. On the ground, there was more and more evidence of footprints the further I walked. Examining the trees, there was also evidence of branches cut with axes. Off to the side, there was trash and shell casings. No doubt, I have reached our hunting trail.

Home. I am finally almost home.

As I limped closer towards the sun beams, a million thoughts crossed my mind. What should I do first? How do I explain everything that happened to us in the trailer park? How do I explain this beast wasn't a beast at all? Just a human, a murderous human. Were there others like him out there?

The forest finally cleared. I rested against a sturdy tree to catch my breath. Off in the distance, I saw a search party from camp rushing towards the woods. I couldn't tell if my compatriots saw me, so I raised my arm to wave. As I waved, it was the first time I realized I never put my gun in my holster this whole time.

∗∗∗

Bears don't shoot guns. At least no bear that I know of. The old man was wrong, but he was too focused on finding the source of the gunshot to even explain himself. No one was asking any questions anymore. The search party became dead silent as we made our way towards the woods. Looking at their faces, it was hard to tell if they were more focused or terrified. I was gripping my gun so tight that I lost feeling in my hands.

None of this is making any sense. Who outside of our camp has guns?

As kids, we were told there we found all the survivors that we would ever find. After the war, the elders would tell us that a disheveled wanderer would come in from time to time. We would give them food and shelter; some stayed while others tried to continue their journey alone. Usually, we'd find those travelers' bodies in the woods, half-eaten by the foxes. By the time I was born, no one else ever came to the camp. So, we stopped looking. There was no point.

But now we're hearing gunshots in the woods. The search party tried to find the source of the gunshot, but we couldn't find anything other than humans walking in the woods. Definitely no sign of a beast. If it's not a bear or a yeti, what else could it be? Right now, a vengeful ghost sounded the most plausible.

Just when I couldn't be any more confused by the situation, the old man finally spoke. "Everyone split up. Take an entrance to the woods. If you see anything, report back immediately. We have no idea what we're dealing with, so no one, and I mean no one, be a hero out there."

***

It was getting dark, and it did not appear that the group could see me. Try as I might, they couldn't see me waving. I don't know if I have the energy to keep walking. I tried to yell, but nothing came out. My throat was too hoarse from all the traveling, so I lost my voice.

I could hear the shouting, but I couldn't make out what they said. Are they coming towards me? No, they appear to be splitting up. At this rate, they may never see me.

Not knowing what else to do, I pulled the trigger.

***

"What the hell was that? The gun shot is now closer." I held out my gun in front of me. Ready to shoot at any movement. My barrel was shaking. Sweat was blurring my vision. My heart was racing, jumping out of my chest. The atmosphere felt like boulders on my shoulders. Each step I took my legs became heavier. Something was rustling the bushes. The sound was faint, but it was definitely nearby. I approached until I could see the outline of something standing by the tree. It wasn't clear, but it appeared that this shadow was holding the gun that was just shot.

I crouched down, pointing my rifle at the figure. If it so much as moves funny, I'll shoot. I swear I'll shoot it.

After having my sights on the figure, I took a deep breath. I wanted to see if it could speak.

"Identify yourself! Keep your hands where I can see them!"

***

The gunshot worked. I just now needed to get the party's attention. I tried yelling my name, to let the boy know that I am from the camp. The noise that came out was hoarse and strained, and it came out more like a growl. I saw that the kid jumped. I heard a click. I think I spooked him and he's pointing his gun at me. Without the ability to talk, my options are limited. I'm going to have to walk towards him. I began limping towards him. Realizing that walking with a gun in my hand will be seen as a threat, I tossed my gun aside.

BANG!

BANG!

***

The figure fell in a heap. My ears were ringing, which made it hard to tell if the figure was dead or not. I sat still, pointing my gun in direction, waiting for any sign of life. No movement. I slowly stood up, making sure to never take my eyes off the figure. Once I was upright, I checked my body to make sure I wasn't hit. I slowly started to inch my way towards the figure. The closer I got, the better I could hear faint gasping for air. I stood over the figure. Like everyone speculated, it was a beast. Covered in mud and blood. Coughing up blood, trying to will his way back up to finish his mission.

"You thought that you could come to my camp and kill everyone? How many of our search party did you kill already? Guess what? This is where you die."

I spat on him and cocked my rifle.

***

Why can't this boy recognize me? I have seen him around the camp. I even taught him how to hold his rifle.

Stop. You know me. I am one of you.

It was no use. I knew it, but I tried anyway. My voice was already gone, and now I was gurgling blood. If he couldn't understand me before he shot me, there was no hope in him understanding me now. Plus, he is standing over me, with a gun pointed in my face.

I desperately tried looking directly into his eyes. I thought that maybe he'd wake up and actually see who he was pointing a gun at. Instead, the closer I looked at him, the more I realized he was a frightened boy. Why wouldn't he be? He's not thinking straight. If the rest of the group doesn't come and stop him, I am a dead man.

As my life flashed before my eyes, for whatever reason, I thought about the man I killed in the trailer park. Maybe, it was right for me to kill him. After all, I killed my crew. But I went overboard humiliating him and refusing to bury him. Looking

23

back, he looked just as frightened as the boy standing over me. I didn't know his age, but I remember him looking about ten years younger than me. If that's the case, while I was fighting in that pointless war, he might have been growing up in the middle of it. Maybe his house was bombed, maybe his entire town was wiped out in an instant. Both parents were gone in an instant, and he had no one to look after him. But he somehow survived, and he somehow learned to fend for himself. A bombed-out trailer park wasn't a bad idea for a shelter now that I think about it.

What if he explored a little farther than he did? Maybe he would've found our camp. Maybe we would've taken him in.

Maybe I wouldn't be lying on the ground after fighting and killing you.

I looked around for the rest of the search party. They were running towards us, but they're not going to make it in time. The boy cocked his gun. I looked in his eyes one last time and the fire. The same fire I had not that long ago.

***

The old man screamed as loud as his voice would allow him to.

"Stop! What the hell are you doing? Stand down! That man you're pointing a gun at is—"

Bang!

About the Author

Haven Shin explores the line between humanity and the wilderness, a key theme that is evident. His stories often take place in harsh, fragmented landscapes, illustrating how distorted perceptions of reality can lead to order descending into violence. In doing so, his writing is quite unsettling. Shin's literary style is known for combining visceral, sensory images and lots of layers of narrative voice. He wants readers to think about what it is that makes us human and what is inhuman, and *Beasts of Man* explores this path, pondering the monsters we create in others and within ourselves.